THE COOKIE CUTTER HOUSE

THE COOKIE CUTTER HOUSE

JOCELYN G. DONAHOO

Mildred,
Come to God for great blessings. He won't steer you wrong. Keep the faith.
Jocelyn G. Donahoo

Printed by CreateSpace, an Amazon.com Company

Cover by Alaina Nicole

Author photo by Sharon Brown-Halmon

Acknowledgements

I would like to thank Jesus Christ for illuminating this gift of writing to me; my mother, Pauline Elizabeth Foster, for her selfless sacrifice and "don't quit" spirit; my husband Carl, for having faith in me and pushing me toward overcoming my doubts and fears, being my sounding board, lay editor, manager, and book seller, even before it went into print; my sister, Alisa Kuumba, for putting me in touch with my editor, Freedom, who made suggestions to improve my story, and rescued me from formatting; Pastor Darrell Coleman's "Stay Focused on your Destiny" and Bishop John Pace II's "You Have What it Takes" faith building sermons; Alaina Johnson for making my friend, Rhonda Trueman's vision into an awesome cover; Dr. Hunt, my mentor, who encouraged and taught me the fundamentals of poetry and storytelling. I'm still learning. There are a plethora of family and friends, too many to name, but you know who you are, who encourage my writing.

Thank you.

"Babies, GOD'S VISION that life MUST go on."

Carl T. Donahoo, Jr.

March 14, 2013

"These are *not* my breasts!" I said hovering over Dustin, water droplets rolling off my skin onto him and the bed.

Dustin scooted over and questioned my sanity for running out of the shower soaking wet. But my hands didn't lie. Something had changed. And I was afraid to find out what. Do I have breast cancer? After common sense deliberation and two pregnancy tests, ends up I was pregnant. We'd been so careful. I wanted children, but down the line. I was on my career track as an Engineer with the Air Force Civilian PALACE Acquire Program. Dustin, on the other hand, was ecstatic. He kissed me and tenderly placed his hand just below my navel. Our eyes met and his sunny smile made *me* excited.

"We're going to have a baby!" I gushed.

That was months ago. And that's what prompted Dustin and I on our quest to find a space big enough to accommodate the baby. We'll see how it goes.

March 15, 2013

We went cyber and house hunting and couldn't agree on the type of home. Dustin told the realtor I thought one of the ranch style houses was too *redneck*. Just because he grew up in the country, doesn't mean I want to. I told her I want a *cookie cutter* house. Dustin says it's because I'm an Air Force brat used to living in base housing. What did I expect!

We're from two different realms.

The homes we saw were either above Dustin's price point or had obsolete white appliances, small rooms, wallpaper . . . need I go on?

March 23, 2013

Today in the realtor's office, Peyton repositioned making my lopsided belly look like a mini basketball rolling through pantyhose, and her proud daddy said, "Whoa! Did you see my football player?"

But I corrected him with, "No, *she* did a somersault."

We chose not to know the baby's sex, and I'm having some uncertainty. It's kind of hard to buy clothes and decorate not knowing. My daughter's room could be pink or lavender, and she could have frilly clothes. I wonder if she'll have Dustin's reddish blonde hair. I doubt it'll be straight like his. Not with my bushy hair in the mix.

Home hunting was a bust. We're anxious to depart from apartment living. After spending four years in college dorms and apartments, with the noisy partying and thin walls, we want a single-family dwelling.

April7, 2013

Woo-hoo! We found a renovated stucco home with ample space between the neighbors. It has three bedrooms, stainless steel appliances, granite countertops, and the big backyard that needs some landscaping made Dustin's eyes light up. That should meet his need for a fixer-upper. Mentally, I had the couch by the window, and the chair juxtaposed until Dustin said, "Stop daydreaming about arranging the furniture. It's priced higher than we wanna spend." He's right. Since I'll be home with the baby for at least her first year, we need to stay on budget. Outside, there was an Asian guy mowing his lawn, and a mixed group of boys shooting hoops on a garage rim. Living in a culturally diverse neighborhood is important to us. Because of my military upbringing, I'm used to different types of people and all kinds of cuisine. Dustin on the other hand, calls himself a redneck and proud of it. His dad's a plumber. If he and his family aren't fishing, they're hunting. I recall the time Dustin came home from bow hunting with his face camouflaged just like his outfit. He scared the living daylights out of me. He better be glad he hadn't taught me how to shoot yet. Maybe we can talk the owner down on the price of the house.

June 1, 2013

I don't know which side of the family is worse with their incendiary statements. Today at the baby shower, Dustin's Aunt Sally, still looks and treats me like I've got smallpox. And when all of his family had left, Dominique, a bank vice president asked me, "How could you sell out and marry a white boy? And then he has the nerve to expect you to forfeit your degree, and have you at home serving him. Slavery was abolished!"

Before I could even defend Dustin and I, Auntie Eunice said, "Stop talking to your cousin like that. You're just mad she has a man who loves and takes care of her. Which is more than you have. Maybe if you'd open yourself up, you could have a man, too. But you have that long list of unrealistic qualifications."

I was happy my parents told me to find a good, decent, Christian man. As long as a black man was in the mix of consideration, they didn't care. Before I got married, Mama schooled me.

"Every day somebody is going to try to make you feel like you made the wrong choice. It's hard to *stay* married. With your *own* kind. Period. So, as long as you and Dustin are strong, you'll make it. Just remember, marriage is work. But more importantly, divorce is *not* an option."

She and Daddy have been together for 30 years with us moving a lot. I've been to so many schools and had to sever and make new friendships. Daddy went on three remote tours of duty, and numerous TDYs (temporary tours of duties). He even took a tour without us so I could graduate with my friends. Dustin's parents have 28 years under their belts. We both come from good stock.

We received a slew of gifts. Mama bought the car seat, and Ms. Billie, Dustin's mom, bought the rocker. Some people gave me pretty little girl clothes that tugged at my heart. I really want a girl.

June 2, 2013

Peyton is due on the 30th. Dustin promised to take me out to dinner and dancing on the weekend. Maybe I'll get lucky. He's afraid to play anymore; fearful he'll harm the baby. But the doctor told us it's okay to make love. I hope to convince him on the renovated house.

June 8, 2013

The evening started out lovely. The *Blackened Chicken Pasta* I had at *Louie's Pasta* was delicious. As usual, Dustin had *Spaghetti and Meatballs.* He won't even try anything different. He's always saying, "I'm a simple guy." The club was packed, but a couple of guys noticed my belly and gave up their table for me. Dustin and I danced twice, him with his off beat country boy steps, me weighted down with Peyton. He went to the bathroom and LaRon from work came over. "I see you bopping your head, come on," he said, and pulled me up. I was leaning close to his ear to tell him something because the music was so loud. It's crazy, but I knew the instant that Dustin saw me. My senses heightened, chill bumps erupted across my chocolate skin, and I could feel his eyes stabbing me in my back. The man has a strange aura. The negative energy swirled around mixing with *"Cha-cha to the left..."* And the night spun into disaster. He walked up amongst the crowd of people who were turning and I introduced them. People were moving and bumping into us. "Excuse me," hollered a lady old as Mama, who had the nerve to be wearing red stilettos and a red butt cupping mini dress. Beyonce she wasn't. The shocked look on LaRon's face spoke volumes, and because Dustin looked anything but friendly with that nefarious scowl on his face, LaRon excused himself. Quickly. Dustin accused me of flirting. He all but snatched me off the dance floor. Aunt Eunice had cautioned me that jealousy wasn't as cute as I thought it was. Tonight I understood what she meant.

The waitress came to the table, and Dustin ordered "two tequila shots", which he downed consecutively upon receiving, and then slammed down his glass. An argument pursued when I asked for the keys to drive home. "I can drive my own wife home," his yell fading in the loud music. The middle child, I was always the mediator. But with Dustin, he wasn't hearing anything logical. He's simple all right. At least he was simple enough to let me drive us home.

June 9, 2013

Dustin's retched, day old, fermenting fruity breath, infused the room. Indisputably, there was no playing last night. His fumbling advances were rejected. And he had the audacity to admonish me with his inebriated slur, "I know you want a brotha. You can be mad if you want to, but di-vorce is not an op-tion." I couldn't believe he accused me of wanting a black guy, any guy. Please. Although LaRon is tall and handsome with a cinnamon complexion, I don't want him. He doesn't have anything over Dustin. Okay, so he does have that Taylor Lautner *Twilight* physique.

I flashed back to working on a group project for Professor Fleischer's class, when Dustin didn't have his assignment. He was the weakest link. Everyone else had left the conference room pissed, and we went back and forth.

"What is your problem?" I asked.

He retorted with, "Problem. Natalie, *you're* the one with the problem."

"Me! You don't have the research you were assigned."

"Unlike yur spoiled, proper talking tight ass, I work two jobs *and* go to school. " Spoiled? My brother Andre is the spoiled brat in our family. Dustin's country-drawl "yur" vs. "your" butt had a lot of gall. Was he calling me uppity?

I remember standing up and pointing my finger in his face saying, "You don't know anything about me."

He stood up making me look like Jada Pickett Smith facing off Chris "Birdman" Anderson.

"No?" He lightly swatted my finger. "Keep your hands out my face—what about that Mercedes you drive?"

"Not that it's any of your business."

It's old. Daddy had bought it when we were stationed in Germany because it's a lot cheaper there. But I wasn't going to tell him that.

"I'm not going to entertain anymore of your bullshit!"

"Oh, the lil princess is cursing," he whined, his hands trembling in a stop position, his shoulders hunched, "I'm scared."

The librarian came into the room and shushed us. We glowered at each other, his yellow-brown lion eyes against my dark chocolate ones, veins popping out of our necks, my head rocking, that little twitchy kiss-like thing he does with his lips. Then he burst out laughing and that infuriated me even more.

"What—is—so—funny?" I said.

And he bent over busting a gut, tears shedding and hiccupping. "You . . . us."

He looked and sounded so ridiculous, a giggle broke out of me. We ended up getting a bite to eat at McDonald's amidst some disparaging eyes, and apologizing for our angry outbursts. However, I held him accountable to his word on the project. That was the start of our relationship. He makes me so mad, but God I love that man.

June 12, 2013

I'm scared. Peyton was due on June 30th, but I'm in real labor. Guilt is creeping through my veins about my first child, whom I allowed to be vacuumed out of me when I was only 15. Daddy was in Korea at the time, and neither he nor Dustin knows anything about her. I'm sure it—she, was a girl. I thought I was something dating a senior. Collie played me, told me he loved me, and I believed him. I gave him my most precious gift on the beach, and he trampled all over it. He emptied his waste in me and was off to his next conquest. I never told Collie or my sister, Bria. Only Mama. She was upset but more understanding than I deserved, and helped me make the most difficult decision of my life. I considered having the baby, putting it up for adoption, and getting rid of it. My decision still haunts me to this day, but I was selfish. I didn't want to give up the debate team, volleyball, the Key Club, and chorus. I was a teenager. Being on the debate team helped me obtain my full ride at the University of Florida where I met Dustin.

The last few days have been awful. Dustin and I have been curt to each other. We hate to hold grudges and yet, we've been quietly dining, watching TV apart, and me rubbing my own belly vs. cuddling. Negative thoughts of identity crisis: being forced to choose a race, the whole light skin, dark skin dilemma in the black community; discrimination and disparagement in the mainstream society, keeps intersecting my mind, making me nervous about bringing a mixed child into the world. So many people, even our own families question our intentions. Oooh! That was a sharp one. I'll check in later. I'm afraid to bring this baby into the world.

June 13, 2013

Dustin apologized and admitted he was jealous. "I'm just a simple redneck," he said, and kissed my forehead. I pulled his cheeks closer and softly pressed my lips to his. "And I wouldn't want you to be anything else. I love *you*." That man, my husband, stood by my side, coached my breathing and breathed right along with me, rubbed my back, gave me ice chips, walked me to the bathroom, around the hall, and encouraged me through the worst pain I've ever endured. And when he cut his son's umbilical cord with damp eyes, I never loved him more.

Peyton is very light, but the tips of his ears are tan. I can't really tell what color his puffy eyes are. His hair is light brown, but there's no denying who his daddy is. He does that little pouty thing Dustin does with his lips. Incredible. Daddy hugged Dustin and thanked him for his first grandchild, especially since Bria and Andre are single, 30 and 25, and career oriented. Dustin hugged him stiffly and said, "Thank you, sir." He's never quite gotten over Daddy introducing me to one of his junior officers after I invited Dustin to dinner. He's worried he doesn't measure up to Daddy's high standards, and claims that's why I'm such a tight-ass. He's 27, has had three raises since he started the Air Force Civilian PALACE Acquire Program, and is in line for the Lead Systems Analyst position. Mama on the other hand, is his girl. She insists he call her mom and is always cooking something special for him.

When Dustin announced our engagement to his parents, I was nervous, but his father, Papa Owen, spoke candidly. "Some of our extended family may have issue," but he assured me with a hug, "You're gonna be my daughter, and they better respect you."

And Ms. Billie, his mother echoed, "Or they're not welcome here."

Later that night Dustin told me, "See, I told you they were crazy about you."

I hope they're ready.

June 22, 2013

Dustin emptied boxes and put some books on the bookcase. Then asked me, "Hear that?" I said, "Hear what?" and he said, "Exactly." We mirrored a smile. It was quiet, no boom-boom through the walls. Dustin's astute negotiating skills won us the bid on the renovated house for the selling price, and the owner paid all the closing costs. Only Peyton's room is completely arranged. Dustin is cooking, cleaning, and unpacking. He told me, "You just worry about taking care of my son." Sitting on the couch in the living room with Peyton latched onto my breast, I pointed, "Okay then, please hang our family pictures on that wall.

July 8, 2013

OMG! Peyton is more than a notion. Just when I think I can get something done, he starts wailing. Now I know why I was selfish. At 15, there is no way I could've made it. Everything was hunky-dory as along as Dustin was at home doing everything. But now he's back at work. His mom wanted to help, but she's the dispatcher for their plumbing business. Mama, too but she and Daddy had already paid for their Alaskan cruise. This boy is greedy. And now that his father knows he's only got two more weeks, he's been sniffing around. I need to fill my birth control prescription. Dustin doesn't want me to. He says he doesn't want his son messed up. Me either, but I definitely don't want back-to-back stair-step children. The research shows breastfeeding's safe as long as the milk supply has been established. We're going to have to be very careful. Mama said that that old wives' tale about breastfeeding being good birth control is a myth. Two of my uncles are proof of that.

July 13, 2013

It's Peyton's one month birthday. Because Mama is old school, and says you have to wait six weeks, I haven't had him out around *"all those germs."* To celebrate, Dustin took us shopping and out to our favorite wing restaurant. The game was interrupted with a breaking news bulletin. Dustin and I watched as the verdict came down. And the next thing I know, a roar of cheers rang out. We couldn't believe it. That jury voted "not guilty" for that wannabe cop George Zimmerman, and the smiling faces of George, his family, and his defense team seemed to be on every TV. Furious, I stood up and shouted "Really? A 17-year-old-boy is dead!" Dustin holding Peyton with one arm jerked me down and had the audacity to look embarrassed. And when I asked him why he did that, he said he didn't want to have to kick somebody's ass. I went off and told him, "The man profiled and followed a 17-year-old-boy with a loaded, no clipped gun, with intent to kill, *after* the dispatcher distinctly told him not to pursue. And he did just that. Killed him." Dustin told me to calm down. Calm down! I couldn't bite my tongue when I told him, "There's no justice for black people in America." My cell started beeping with all kinds of messages. Everybody was in shock. Even my NRA loving friends. And to think we were supposed to be stopping over to Dustin's Fox Network—Rush Limbaugh supporting family's house. I wasn't in the mood. He tried whispering his warm breath in my ear with "Come on Nat", but it didn't work this time. He claimed we had to at least show our face, and then we could leave. Yeah, until he got involved in one of those dumb street fighting games. Then Peyton and I could be there all night. And my name is Natalie.

July 14, 2013

Dustin kept turning on the TV to all the different pundit perspectives. We totally disagree. He said he and his family are hunters. They disagree with

President Obama about registering their guns or changing the *stand your ground law*.

Dustin complained, "They just want to take our guns and our rights that people fought and died for. I sure as hell will stand my ground if somebody tries to harm you, my son, or tries to break in this house!"

I tried to make him see they don't want gun owners to relinquish their guns. They just don't want guns to fall into any fool's hands the way they did with that psycho who walked up into Sandy Hook Elementary School, and shot and killed all of those innocent children and teachers.

Dustin hollered, "That was an anomaly."

"You're new to this racism thing," I pointed out.

His face turned red when he said, "Oh yeah?" veins popping out of his neck, "You think I haven't experienced racism? I don't know how many times I went to the gym to play basketball, and nobody gave me any play, because I was *white*!"

I came back with, "Now you know how *we* feel. We have a mixed son, and you're going to have to deal with more than just judgmental looks and hand-shielded whispers. Peyton could've been Trayvon Martin!"

As if he objected, Peyton started crying. I got up and Dustin argued, "We're not finished," as I darted down the hall into Peyton's room. After picking him up, I changed Peyton's saturated diaper, sat down in the comfortable rocker Ms. Billie gave us, lifted my tank top, and before I could get settled, Peyton nudged around like a bobble-head searching for my nipple. That always makes us smile.

Dustin walked in and I watched his stormy face melt into a grin as Peyton found his target and started suckling. Nothing like a child to bring two opinionated strong willed parents into submission by watching their son with joy. Dustin apologized and I did too. Reluctantly. We can't let racism ruin our lives.

July 15, 2013

Dustin and I have been walking on eggshells over the Trayvon Martin issue, neither one of us wanting to wreck our thin reconciliation. We plan on having a house warming party in a few weeks. We just need to get the last of our boxes put up, and add those finishing touches that make a house a home. Dustin wanted to put a deer head over the mantle. Is he crazy? First of all, that is straight country-redneck. I asked him how he could kill Bambi, and he said he never kills for the sport of it, only for the food. Then he called me out and said, "What's the big deal? You eat," then counted on his fingers, "fish, chicken, beef, pork, *and* lamb. So don't act all tight-ass with me. Like you don't enjoy the venison sausage."

I hate to admit when he's right, but he does have a point. The man makes some slamming sausage. I hate to look at those Bambi's eyes. It reminds me of the movie *Powder* where Sean Patrick Flanery makes a character feel the fear and pain of a dying deer. I told Dustin to put it in his man cave.

July 16, 2013

Dustin just gave me a kiss that almost made me forget we had two more weeks before intimacy. I miss him and I know he misses me. His dad and uncle called, and when they mentioned fishing, Dustin's eyes lit up. He tried to deny he wanted to go, but I shooed him off.

When he first showed me off at his family's fish fry, I knew then and there by the open mouth looks and raised eyebrows that I received, Dustin hadn't told anybody about me. His dad bent over backwards trying to help me feel comfortable, and his mom pulled me in the kitchen with some of the women. After a quick demonstration of how she wanted it cut, she set me up with chopping the cabbage for the coleslaw. Dustin, his dad, and some of the men were out on the deck drinking beer and frying mullet. His father has a secret breading that he uses. All I can guess is the jalapenos that he puts in the hushpuppies. Whatever it is, everything was delicious. The thought of it is making my mouth water. I've got that tingling feeling. The milk is filling in my breast and that means one thing, Peyton will be crying any minute.

❖⌘❖

Dustin came home unusually quiet. He pecked me and went out to the garage. I found him descaling the fish, doing that pouty lip thing he does. When I asked him what was wrong, he said, "You don't wanna know."

I told him, "Well, whatever it is you're not very happy about it. Tell me."

He sighed and divulged that his uncle made a humorless crack. I took it to mean he said something racist. Dustin wouldn't say what it was, only that whatever was said was a bad joke.

He left it at that, and I didn't push him. He was pretty upset. Surprisingly, I wrapped my arms around his waist, and told him to forgive him and move on. Then I left him to his thoughts.

I had my own thoughts. It was Easter Eve and the whole family was sitting around the dining room table, undertaking our family tradition of coloring eggs. The contrasting aromas of tempting ham and sulfuric greens cooking hovered in the air. When I brought Dustin home to meet my family, I'd already let them know he was white.

Bria winked and mouthed, "He's cute."

Andre complimented him saying, "Those are some nice kicks," and asked, "Where'd you get them?"

Daddy grilled him like a prosecutor.

Dustin thinks it was because he's white, but Daddy has always grilled my new, no, any of my boyfriends.

Daddy asked, "What church do you attend?"

"Persimmon Baptist Church, sir."

"What's your major?"

"Information Technology, sir."

"What are your five-year career goals?"

"Graduate, secure a position with the government or a fortune 500 company, get my master's in Systems Technology, gain enough experience to become a supervisor, and ultimately own my own business, sir."

I'd heard it a thousand times.

"What are your intentions regarding my daughter?"

"I love her and plan to marry her."

I almost keeled over when he said that. Mama smiled. Bria and Andre drew their heads back, looked at me, and I lifted my hands and shook my head "no." That was the first I'd ever heard.

"What's the deal on the pickup truck?" Referring to the oversize tires, gun rack and "mullet fear me" bumper sticker.

Dustin answered, "Because I'm a redneck, sir" shocking all of us, but breaking the ice.

Everybody except Dustin and Daddy fell out laughing. Daddy just smirked. Mama called Daddy out saying something like "I guess you've met your match. He's career oriented; working two jobs *and* going to school, says he loves our daughter and eventually wants to marry her. And to top it off, he's not afraid to man up and has a sense of humor." She faced Dustin and said, "Dustin, don't mind him. He means well. He's just trying to protect his daughter."

A straight-faced Dustin eyed Daddy and said, "I can respect that, sir." He and Daddy have so much in common. They are both overachievers and believe in defending what's theirs, especially their women and children. I love Daddy and I love Dustin even more.

July 17, 2013

Dustin came to bed pensive last night. He usually plays *Candy Crush* on his phone, but he lay awake staring at the ceiling. I asked if he forgave his uncle yet, and he turned towards me and said, "I love you *so* much, and it hurts me when people refuse to see all your incredible qualities that I was attracted to. The tight-ass ones aside."

I punched him in the arm, and he gave an empty smile. Maybe we should've seriously thought about getting married. I don't want him or I to have to fight this uphill battle our entire marriage. With people who are our family and friends.

Then he turned towards me and said emphatically, "We're in this for the long haul," tapped my chest, "you", then tapped his own, "and me."

It reminded me of our wedding vows. He said "in sickness and in health", and followed it with "forever and ever". And when I said my vows, his lion eyes mesmerized mine and he added insistently, "forever and ever" and I smiled and followed suit, "forever and ever."

Andre once told me Dustin treats me like a piece of Waterford crystal. My heart fluttered and I caressed Dustin's cheeks, slowly rested my forehead against his, and nipped his lips. He moaned and deepened the kiss. All I can say is one thing lead to another, and neither one of us has any regrets. It was as if we needed to safeguard our bond to be one. Okay, in my dreams. I did nip Dustin's lips, and he pushed back from me and said, "Stop playin'."

What did his uncle say?

And why is he punishing me?

July 18, 2013

Dustin got home late today. Instead of at least three times, he called me only once. A new project is in the works, so he claims. He's still just answering my questions and offering no real conversation. I don't like the crazy way he keeps staring at Peyton. He's having second thoughts. He doesn't want to deal.

July 19, 2013

At 5:30 Dustin finally remembered to call his wife. There was laughter in the background when he informed me he had an office going away party. I watch *Mad Men*. All I know is he had better come home without lipstick on his collar or smelling like some witch's cologne. I hope he at least remembers his son. If he wants to see a tight-ass, he's going to meet her whenever he gets home.

Peyton woke me up at midnight and his country redneck daddy was nowhere to be found. So, I fixed it so he'd know not to mess with me.

July 20, 2013

Last night, my phone rang and I ignored it. I heard the doorbell ringing and I ignored that, too. If he wanted to ignore me, not talk to me, and avoid coming home, he could stay wherever he was.

The phone rang again, and this time it was Dustin's co-worker telling me he drove Dustin home, and needed me to move whatever I had blocking the door, so my drunk, negligent husband could get in.

Of all the nerve!

I slipped on my pj bottoms and headed for the door. I was the one who moved the dining room chair and stuck it under the knob, but it took work to get it loose. When I finally opened the door, two guys I'd never seen before were holding up Dustin. He was plastered and out for the count. The one named Nick introduced himself and Victor, then asked where I wanted them to unload Dustin. My first thought was "on the couch", but I thought about it and told them the office slash guest room. They helped take off his pants, and I thanked them and told them I could take it from there. On the way out, Nick apologized. It was his last minute going away party, and he wanted to make sure Dustin made it home safely. I told them my name and they both said, "We know who *you* are." Nick added, "Your husband talked about you all—night—long."

Well, well, well, he wasn't lying about the party. I hope he didn't blab all of our dirty laundry. To pay him back, Peyton woke up every two hours.

Today has been hard; Peyton's been fussy since last night, and his drunken father has not been any help lounging around all day. He had the audacity to tell me, "CAN'T YOU KEEP HIM QUIET?" which started up a heated argument. Which then got Peyton started, and we both were extremely sorry.

I could care less that Dustin has a hangover.

July 21, 2013

Dustin was in my face at six o'clock this the morning wanting to talk. Well, Peyton had finally quieted down, and I needed to catch up on *my* sleep. Anyway, I didn't have two words for him. I woke up to a waft of mouthwatering bacon, and shortly afterwards, Dustin brought in a tray of my favorite things for breakfast: bacon, a spinach, mushroom, and artichoke omelet, strawberries with whipped cream, chocolate chip pancakes, orange juice, and a frothy cup of white chocolate caramel cappuccino.

I glanced at the clock and it was 11:00. I'd been sleep for five hours. I puckered my lips to ask about Peyton, and Dustin told me I slept through his last tirade, so he gave him a bottle of Enfamil. My emotions went from feeling hurt and cheated, to having neglected my baby.

So I faulted *Dustin* and said, "You did what? How dare you! Peyton has never had Enfamil befo—"

"And he did just fine," Dustin said just as calm and matter-of-factly at a staccato pace. "Nat, you were exhausted." He sighed, trying to hold back being riled. "I'm not blaming you. Just trying to help."

He helped all right. Suppose Peyton prefers the bottle over me?

My in-laws were on their way over; therefore I had two hours to get myself together. Dustin tried to apologize, but I told him we didn't have time to get into it.

His parents came over and I gave a poor performance. When his mom asked what's wrong, I told her I was tired. That wasn't a lie. I am tired. Tired of their son.

We agreed to go forth with Peyton's christening on the 28th of July. They didn't stay long to allow me time to get my rest. Before they could get out the door good, Dustin apologized for being intoxicated, and promised he wouldn't do it again.

"That's what you said the last time!" I reminded him.

He had the nerve to look frustrated. I'm frustrated. And tired. Tired of him not standing up to his uncle, so I asked him one more time what was said.

He protected his uncle and wouldn't tell me. So I told him, "Next week when you want to relieve some of that tension you keep complaining about, sleep with your uncle."

On that note, I shut down, got up from the couch, and started dinner. Then he yelled that would be incestuous, which didn't even justify a response.

July 22, 2013

My cousin Dominique, is in town for a banker's convention, and wanted to see the baby. I wasn't in the mood for her either. She said the camera didn't do justice to how cute Peyton is. Then she commented on my hair. I usually twist it, let them out, and finger pick it. But I haven't had time for that. It was pulled back in an afro-puff. Dustin likes the let down twists. He says I look like a lion.

Acting like she was criticizing the performance of her subordinates, she gave me the once over, nit-picked my non-made up face, tee shirt, and nylon gym shorts. Then told me, "If you don't want your man stepping out, *you* need to put on some makeup," frowned, "and wear attractive clothes." She, who wears a weave, an overly made up face and designer clothes, has never been married or had any kids, knows?

I looked in the mirror and she had a point. I could at least put on some mascara and lip-gloss. Dustin likes the sexy smoky eyes. Unfortunately, we are back to two ships passing in a night. He claims he'll be working late every day this week.

July 23, 2013

I am stir-crazy. I miss work. I'm not sure how long I'll be able to stay at home. It sounded good, but I'm bored. Don't get me wrong, I love my son, and definitely don't want him at some childcare center, or being watched by some stranger. Speaking of which, Peyton's calling.

❖⌘❖

Dustin got home at 7:00 with his hand behind his back. I could care less what he had. But when he presented a *Publix's* grocery store cellophane package, stalks first, I rolled my eyes, until the most vibrantly beautiful bouquet of golden yellow, red tipped roses, took my breath away. Topped with a heartfelt apology, any anger I had built up dissolved like Kool-Aid in a pitcher of water. Dustin knows how to beg for my forgiveness. Then my man thanked me for taking such good care of his son. I couldn't help but smile. I guess whatever his uncle said, I'll never know. He'll probably be at the christening. Dustin talked about a date night to get me out of the house, and suggested dinner and a movie. I look forward to it.

July 24, 2013

We're trying to mend our fractured relationship. Dustin sat down, pulled me onto his lap, and watched an episode of Iyanla Vanzant's, *Fix My Life.* He even enjoyed it. Peyton started crying, and Dustin asked me to pump milk more often so he can feed his son. He's very hands on. I need to thank his parents for that.

July 25, 2013

Dustin's sister can't make the christening, so he wants to change the date until August 11th. That's fine with me, but I'll have to check with the rest of the family.

July 26, 2013

Date night is finally here. I'm going to have smoky eyes, lioness hair, and wear Dustin's favorite, my turquoise dress that defines my assets. Peyton interrupted me while I was trying to set my hair and it's not ready. I tried on my turquoise dress. Augh, it's too tight! Now what am I going to do? I had a baby. My black & white geometric patterned maxi dress with splashes of golden yellow and rust will just have to do. It should conceal some of my imperfections.

I ended up with a side part and two French braids, and hoped my chandelier earrings and a couple of bangle bracelets would set off my outfit. Walking into the living room, Dustin's lion eyes lit up and he uttered, baby you look beautiful. Mama complimented my Tyra Bankslike smoky eyes. They boosted my confidence because I felt fat.

We made it to the new bistro I've been itching to try. I was looking over the menu when all of a sudden that tingly feeling happened. Dustin asked me what was wrong. I almost panicked fearing I'd have two wet quarter size spots on my breasts. That's when I remembered I was wearing the breast pads, so I was able to deny any problems.

Our food came quickly. I looked at my cell, and Dustin pointed out that was the 3rd time I'd checked the time, shook his head and said, "Peyton's fine."

He called the waiter over and asked to have our food boxed up. I apologized, and told him we could stay. I looked so miserable; he knew I probably couldn't enjoy myself. I'd been looking forward to getting out of the house, but I missed my son. And so did my milk-engorged breasts.

July 27, 2013

Dustin is working on his landscaping project. Even though Peyton is only 6 weeks old, he's making a sandbox. He really has a talent when it comes to yard work and landscaping. I guess being a country boy has its perks. His father is coming over to help him install the sprinkler system. Dustin's planning a water feature, and I'm excited to see how it turns out. I went back in the house to get some lemonade for everybody, when I heard the roar of that red pickup truck pull up in the driveway. Good. Maybe they can get things resolved.

I heard Dustin bark, "What the hell are you doing here?" This to his uncle, who is more like a brother since there're only four years apart.

"Come on Dustin," his Uncle Bo whined. "I apologized. You know we both used to talk like that."

Dustin got defensive. "Used to. Anyway that was before I came to my senses. It's wrong to even joke like that."

Bo inserted his shovel in the firm ground and started digging. He stopped, his eyes looking remorseful. "I was just joking."

Thinking it was safe, I pushed the sliding door further open, headed out towards the patio when I heard Dustin say, "My son is not a mutt!"

I bulldozed my way over towards them like a lioness protecting her cub screaming, "Oh, I've got your mutt!"

Dustin gasped and Bo winced.

I stepped up in Bo's face.

He immediately averted his eyes to Dustin.

Hitting my chest I said, "This high-fa-luting, proper speaking—sista,' can stoop down to your trailer trash, hatemongering level. Because you think—I'm," irrepressible tears escaped my eyes and my voice trembled, "just . . . a nig—"

Dustin dropped his shovel and blurted, "No, Nat, no!" and hugged me.

Bo kept apologizing but I wouldn't acknowledge him.

I broke free from Dustin and said, "Why would you even agree to be Peyton's godfather if that's what you believed? I thought you were my friend. And to think I told Dustin to forgive you. I could just kick myself." Bo's expression shrunk smaller and smaller. Then I

shamed him with, "You sat on my couch, watched my TV, ate my food, laughed and joked with me . . . you are a flip-flopping hypocrite. It's one thing to talk about me," I slapped my chest and spat out, "but my son, who can't even defend himself—just leave!"
Bo opened his mouth, and I dismissed him with my stiff arm—talk to the hand. His face flushed and he gritted his teeth. Then he looked at Dustin, whose hurt eyes deserted him.

So he left.

When we got in the house, I let Dustin have it. I called the both of them a couple of racist rednecks. I accused him of letting me take up for Bo knowing good and well it wasn't even about me, but my son, our son.

Then he said, "I told you, you didn't wanna know."
I slapped him and he grabbed my hand so quickly and with so much anger, I wasn't ready for his retaliation.

July 28, 2013

Bria called and I confided in her about the Bo situation.

"What! Not Bo," she said, just as shocked as we were. "Another undercover racist. They smile in your face and stab you in the back."
Dustin and I are having a hard time trying to replace him as godfather. She suggested our brother, Andre, but he's too immature and selfish. When she added LaRon in the mix, all I could think about is how

insecure Dustin is around him. I'll figure out something, somebody.

After I slapped Dustin yesterday, he snatched my hand, argued he married me and wasn't a racist. Then he smashed me up against him, restrained my flapping hands behind my back, and kissed me until I was dizzy and under submission.

Abruptly, he released me, said, "Racists don't do *that*!" And I was still senseless when he walked out the door.

All that anger, duplicity, and frustration, fueled a romance novel night. Nestled together, Dustin and I had a heart-to-heart talk. I begged him not to keep any secrets even if he thought he was protecting me. He claimed he hates to see that hurt look on my face, but promised we wouldn't have any secrets regardless of the consequences. A kiss sealed our pact to remain a united front.

July 29, 2013

Bo's faux pas spread through the family like a Kardashian story in the media. Rapidly. Mama was hurt. Daddy claimed his first impression and *that* pickup truck said it all. They want to meet with Dustin's family to iron out this mess. And they want to do it before the christening.

Dustin's family had a pow-wow and they're all in. They feel terrible and hope it won't be held against them. When Dustin got that *meek* voice, I knew *something* was up. His dad wants Bo there, as well. I don't. The sight of him makes me want to slap the "mutt" off his tongue. The way I should've done, instead of taking it out on my husband. And that's not all. His father wants us to reconsider Bo as the godfather.

I couldn't believe Dustin even uttered that out of his lips. Before I could stop it, "What! Is he on crack? No way!" slipped off my tongue. "And what happened to you being just as mad as me?" I was on a roll. "They brainwashed you into sticking with your *white redneck* family?"

The wounded look on his face told me I'd gone too far.

"See how easy that diarrhea rolled out of your mouth?" He shook his head, incredulously. "You blacks are always accusing us of being racist! Y'all ain't any better." And with that, he stormed out of the house. Three hours later, he texted me *"spending the night over my parent's house."*

I texted back *"good."* And didn't regret it.

We needed some space.

I kept looking at my phone.

Nothing.

July 30, 2013

I wonder if Dustin slept like a rock like he usually does. I don't know when he came by and got some clothes. That's scary. Somebody came in my house and I didn't even wake up. The alarm was on. He usually kisses me on his way out in the morning. Sometimes I remember, sometimes I think he's lying. Surely I'd wake up if he kisses me. I didn't miss him last night. His son finally had plenty of room in our queen size bed. Everybody called to see how we were doing. I didn't tell them my husband walked out on me. Dustin hasn't called me not once today. At least I didn't have to drop what I was doing to answer the phone.
He didn't come home. The sucker could've had the decency to let me know. It's his loss. I put the spaghetti and meatballs in the freezer.

Okay, it's 7:00 p.m. The big baby ran home to mommy and daddy. What about *his* son?
Mama called. What does she have, ESP? When she asked about Dustin, the suppressed tears couldn't wait to fall. She advised me to suck up my pride and apologize. I balked, but she refused to hear a bunch of stupid excuses. Her words, not mine.

I changed out of my gym shorts and tee shirt, donned my peach strapless sundress, the one he claims shows too much leg—only because I didn't have to iron it.

Ms. Bank Executive would be pleased.

Then I packed up his son. We'll see what happens.

July 31, 2013

When I got to his parent's home, Ms. Billie said, "It's about time *one* of you acted like you've got some sense. He's out on the back porch."

She reached for Peyton in that cumbersome carrier, "I'll take my grandson."

Slipping the diaper bag off my shoulder his father said, "And don't leave this house without him . . . your husband that is. Our grandson can stay as long as he wants."

I should've known I'd find Dustin drowning his sorrows. There he was, sitting on the stump in the yard, a beer can in his hand. At night. In the dark. With the snakes.

I was hesitant to step out there. He looked miserable. And I loved it.

"What are *you* doing here?" he asked, dryly and unanimated. No delight in seeing *me*. Only "Where's *Peyton*?"

My anger gage rose and I almost said, "If you came home where you belong, you'd know." But Mama's advice "Do not start an argument" sat on my shoulders. And because my big mouth is what drove him out in the first place, I uttered, "I don't want to argue."

Did I have to sound so whiney?

He sighed, "Me either."

I asked when he was coming home. And he told me, "Lion hair and smoky eyes won't bring me back."

How dare he know my intentions. He's tired of me giving up on him and our marriage. He insists I need to grow up. Every argument we have, I'm quick to hold grudges. So what, he is too.

I clutched his hand and said, "Let's stop this madness. I love you. Come home."

August 1, 2013

Going to get Dustin backfired. After I practically begged him to come home, he folded his arms, and puckered his pouty lips. He expected an apology. So I caved with a half-hearted "I'm sorry I insulted you and your family. Please come home."

He nodded his head towards me, raised his eyebrows then said, "And?"

So I promised not to drag his family and race in the mud. I held back my true thoughts of "What about you?" but realized he always respects me. Then as Mama would say, "the Holy Spirit quickened me" with my digs about white people. While watching a scary movie, I've said, "A black person knows it's time to *go*, as soon as the first note of the da-dum da-dum music comes on. Only you crazy white folks go and investigate."

After all of my apologizing, Dustin still didn't come home with us. He helped me pack up our son, carried him to the car, kissed and buckled *him* in, said goodnight and watched us drive off. That made for a restless night. Peyton was off his schedule, so I put him in his own bed allowing both of us an attempt at getting some rest.

Today, no call. Just a text for me to kiss Peyton for him. He's making me suffer. I've got to do something. I admit it. I need my husband.

August 2, 2013

Trying to keep my mind busy, I was preparing my grocery and to-do-list list for the house warming party that we're supposedly having next week, when the phone rang. Dustin called to make sure I'd be home. Like clockwork, he arrived at noon on his lunch break. Why did he have to look so handsome? His light beard was now a neatly trimmed mustache and goatee, the collar length hair that daddy had issue with was cut off, and he had on a shirt and tie. I asked why he cut his hair, and he told me he got the Senior Systems

Developer position. I jumped into his arms and congratulated him. I wondered who tied his tie. As if he read my mind, he said, "Mom did it." Then mentioned, "I'm coming home after work," easily as saying, "Pass the remote."

I sat brooding, not trusting the right words to exit my mouth.

He admitted, "I miss you and Peyton."

I finally asked, "What happened to us? We said we wouldn't let race dictate our lives. And look at us—"

He cut me off and said, "It's you. I'm not black and don't know how you feel. We weren't as worried about race before, but now I—we only want the best for our son. We can't keep doing this. We've got to get this thing straight, before Peyton understands and thinks he's dividing us."

I walked into his arms and crumbled. It felt so good to be held. Too proud to admit how much I love and need him, I winked and told him not to make any plans after work, to come straight home.

He spoke emphatically looking down into my eyes, "All jokes aside. We are past all of this craziness. Agreed?"

It was easy for him to say. I almost wavered but said, "Agreed."

August 4, 2013

Mama had Sunday dinner at her house for the racism pow-wow. "I have the seating integrated the way congress *should* be," she announced. "Otherwise, how can we get anything accomplished if we're only sitting with like-minded people?"

I sat comfortably next to Papa Owen and Ms. Billie. Dustin sat next to Mama and Daddy, his tension apparent in his rigid jawline. Bo fidgeted between the chilly atmosphere of Andre and Bria. Mama's chicken and dumplings, string beans with smoky sausage, tossed salad, cornbread, and homemade red velvet cake and homemade vanilla ice cream, had Ms. Billie asking for recipes and Dustin telling me to learn how to make the dumplings.

Post dessert, Mama started the inquiry when she asked Bo straight out, "Why did you call my grandson a mutt?"

He told her, "Peyton is my nephew. I *love* him. He looked at Dustin and me, "Come on y'all. You know how happy I was when he was born—I was just joking."

I spoke honestly and told Bo, "Just like that, I'm supposed to forgive you? It hurts. I will never trust another word that comes out of your mouth."

"I know that's right!" Bria muttered under her breath.

Papa Owen said, "Now Natalie that's extreme."

But I just kept talking. "And I'm definitely not ready to forgive you."

Bria added her two cents, "They always want a break. But they're not quick to give us any."

Mama scolded Bria to stop making snide remarks.

Dustin accepted the apology but skirted forgiveness.

Mama told us she believed Bo was sincere, and told him, "Forgiveness will come in time."

That started the dialog. Andre admitted some of his friends: white and black, call each other the "n" word. None of the rest of us liked that. As far as I'm concerned, he showed his naivety about true race relations.

"I can't stand *or* trust duplicitous people," Bria claimed. "They're just like that old school song *Smiling Faces*—and all the time stabbing you in the back."

"I have some racists in my family," Papa Owen interjected. "But Bo is not one of them. He made a bad joke."

"O—K," Bria said, and pointed her index finger accusingly, "So, did *you* think it was funny?" When he hesitated, Bria took that as a "yes," crossed her arms and smirked.

Bo sat steaming. His eyes were red and he kept gritting his teeth. He was holding back.

"No," Dustin said, taking up for his dad. "He was mad too. It was Dad who made Bo apologize—"

"*Made* is the key word," Bria pointed out. "Bo didn't see anything wrong with what he said."

Between clenched teeth, Bo said, "*I* made a mistake. Don't take it out on Owen!" He got up from the table.

"What are you doing?" Papa Owen asked.

"I'm outta here," Bo said.

"Good riddance," Bria smarted off.

"How are you going to get anything resolved?" Ms. Billy said to Bo's back, because he was storming out.

"Let him go," Papa Owen said waving his hand, resigned. "Expecting Bo to stay here was futile in this hostile environment."

I was happy Bo left. In fact, the only ones looking regretful were his family.

Then I told Papa Owen, "Well, I appreciate you and Ms. Billie for at least, being *upfront* and honest about it. And accepting me into the family."

Dustin gave a crooked smile at Mom and Dad, and *she* reciprocated.

Daddy replied with a silent, stony stare. Any headway they'd made had now relapsed.

Ms. Billie apologized and asked that we not hold this against them. Daddy and Bria's judgmental sideway glance to each other didn't require a response. They were not sold.

After it was all said and done, our families were polarized.

August 8, 2013

We were just finishing up dinner when the phone rang. Dustin picked it up and was saying, "Wha—Oh, no! What happened?" He listened attentively. "Ok, I'll be right there."

I saw the fear in Dustin's eyes and worried something bad happened to one of his parents. As I blurted, "What happened? Dustin hollered, "Bo was in an accident!"

Dustin was messed up, so I got Mama to watch Peyton. I couldn't let him drive. We went down to Sacred Heart Hospital in Sandestin. The sight of the sight of Bo's deformed leg, bandage covering it or not, sent chills down my spine. Ironically, when we walked in, Bo in obvious agony: teeth clenched, brows furrowed, and grimacing—no happy-go-lucky smile, apologized. As mad as I was, I never wanted any harm to come his way. We told him not to worry about it. This is the wrong time for all of that. Concentrate on getting better. I forgave him and so did Dustin.

It was hard to see Bo the prankster down. Some drunken fool on the bay rammed his boat into Bo's jet ski, crushed Bo's leg, resulting in a compound tibia fracture. Thank God Bo's all right. He's thankful he was able to twist his jet ski. Otherwise, he might have been doomed.

Ms. Billie, Papa Owen, Bo's friend, and family congregated in the waiting room. Because everybody looked so worried, I lead the group in prayer. That's when I remembered and shared Bo's shaving cream prank on a dozing Dustin. That started up the many "Bo" anecdotes. Laughing took off some of the stress until Bo came out of surgery. We saw him briefly after the recovery room and left.

August 9, 2013

It was hard for us to fall asleep. Bo's friend's recount of the accident keeps sending chills down my spine. Of course, I had to *Google* an image. And that image of a bone sticking up out of the skin like a broken chicken leg, haunted me all night long. Dustin pondered what the surgeon had spoken of. Compartment syndrome. A serious complication caused where there's no blood flow because of excessive swelling. Worse case scenario, there could be permanent nerve and muscle damage. That would be devastating. Bo was, I mean, *is* very athletic. Neither Dustin nor I could believe that Bo, suffering a seriously broken leg, was worried about apologizing to us. I actually felt guilty. Outside of the "mutt" incident, Bo had been nothing but fun, loyal, and would give you the shirt off his back. That was an awful thing to happen to anybody. Especially him. We cancelled the party and christening. We've been at the hospital. Bo is in a lot of pain. I've been pumping milk for Peyton so Mama can have some on hand while we're at the hospital.

August 11, 2013

At church today, the day we were supposed to have Peyton's christening, the minister talked about forgiveness highlighting "**Colossians 3:13** "Bear with each other and forgive one another if any of you has a grievance against someone. Forgive as the Lord forgave you" and "**Luke 6:37** "Do not judge, and you will not be judged. Do not condemn, and you will not be condemned. Forgive, and you will be forgiven" from the (NIV) bible.

Dustin and I were both squirming in our seats, because we knew the message was for us. Instead of going 40 minutes down the road, we'd chosen a local church. I'm usually the one who talks about the message, but Dustin led the discussion. We agreed that life is too short for holding grudges. We said we forgave Bo, but did we really?

September 15, 2013

Peyton Idris Pierce was christened today. We decided to have the house warming party after church. And it was Mama's idea to have the parents pay for Aunt Eunice, her sister, to cater it. The food was off the chain good! BBQ ribs, fried fish and hush puppies, grilled shrimp, greens, baked beans, stuffed mushrooms, 7-layer salad, coleslaw, potato salad, Little Smokies, fruit kabobs, chips and dip, cheese and crackers, and a veggie tray. I was so happy none of us had to prepare anything.

Everyone complimented us on the landscaping, especially the little feature pond with the waterfall. Our yard does look like something out of a magazine. I can't begin to name the assortment of ornamental grass and pretty, colorful flowering plants. I proudly gave credit where credit was due to Dustin and Papa Owen. They grinned with their chests poked out.

Some of the pictures and videos we took of Ms. Billie's silly clues, and untimely pauses in the board game Taboo, Daddy's petty nitpicking competition with Dustin on the horseshoe toss, and my outlandish ideas in the game Apples to Apples were hilarious! I perused the pictures and stopped at the one on the altar. It was my idea to reinstate Bo as the godfather, which got some conflicting reactions. Bria was shocked. She put her hand on my forehead, and asked me if I'd lost my marbles picking a racist for Peyton's godfather. Daddy stressed we didn't have to do it because we felt guilty. And in fact, when I broached the subject with Bo, he was full of pride and said, "No. I don't want your pity."

I huffed and rolled my eyes at Dustin, and he told Bo about church. Boy, this Christian walk is more than a notion. Frustrated, I pointed my finger and said, "Listen Bo—"

"Nat," Dustin warned.

"We are not going to beg! If you don't w— "

"Only if yur absolutely sure," Bo said, looking skittish. "I appreciate the opportunity . . . I'll—I'm gonna make you proud."

We received a Bass Pro Shop and other unique gift cards, but the greatest gift we got was when Aunt Eunice's assistant had all of us gather together; Bo with leg brace and crutches; Dustin holding Peyton; Bria and Daddy stiff and standoffish, and everybody else cheesing for our family picture. I titled it *The Cookie Cutter House.* I couldn't help but smile. Hmm, we're anything but.

The Cookie Cutter House Discussion Questions

1. The premise of the story is about a biracial couple having a baby, and a family member making a racial slur. Do you have a problem with miscegenation? Why or why not? Is it okay for certain races to mix vs. others? Do you have historical reasons for disliking the mixing of blacks and whites?

2. Natalie had fears of bringing a mixed child into the world: the light skin, dark skin issues in the black community, and disparagement in mainstream American society. Were her fears warranted or unjustified?

3. Both Bo and Dustin had a history of making racist remarks jokingly. Did it make them racist? Owen, Dustin's father, admitted they had racists in the family, evidenced by Aunt Sally. Is that tolerable? Better yet, have you ever made bigoted remarks? If so, have you gotten angry when one is made about your race? Is it fair to tease certain races and not others?

4. Natalie chose to stay at home with her baby for his first year of life. Was it okay for her to put her own career on hold for her baby? Was her cousin wrong for implying Dustin had Natalie at home "serving him," or saying, "Slavery was abolished?"

5. Dustin allowed his wife to get some much-needed sleep, and in turn, gave Enfamil to Peyton? Was it right or wrong? Would you have been angry or appreciative?

6. Forgiveness is a theme throughout the story. Dustin, Natalie and her family had issues with Bo's remark, and Dustin with Natalie's insult to him and his family. Could you forgive a family member for making a prejudiced remark?

7. Can you think of an instance in your life where forgiveness was difficult? Did the Holy Spirit quicken you to forgive?

8. Was the story believable? Did it challenge your opinion on certain issues?

9. Which scene was most memorable? Who was your favorite character?

10. Was the ending predictable?

"Overall the story is really colorful. I enjoyed meeting the characters, they seemed real and I wanted to know more about them. I liked the humor that was weaved in the story."

Jenelle Davis

Made in the USA
Charleston, SC
21 July 2014